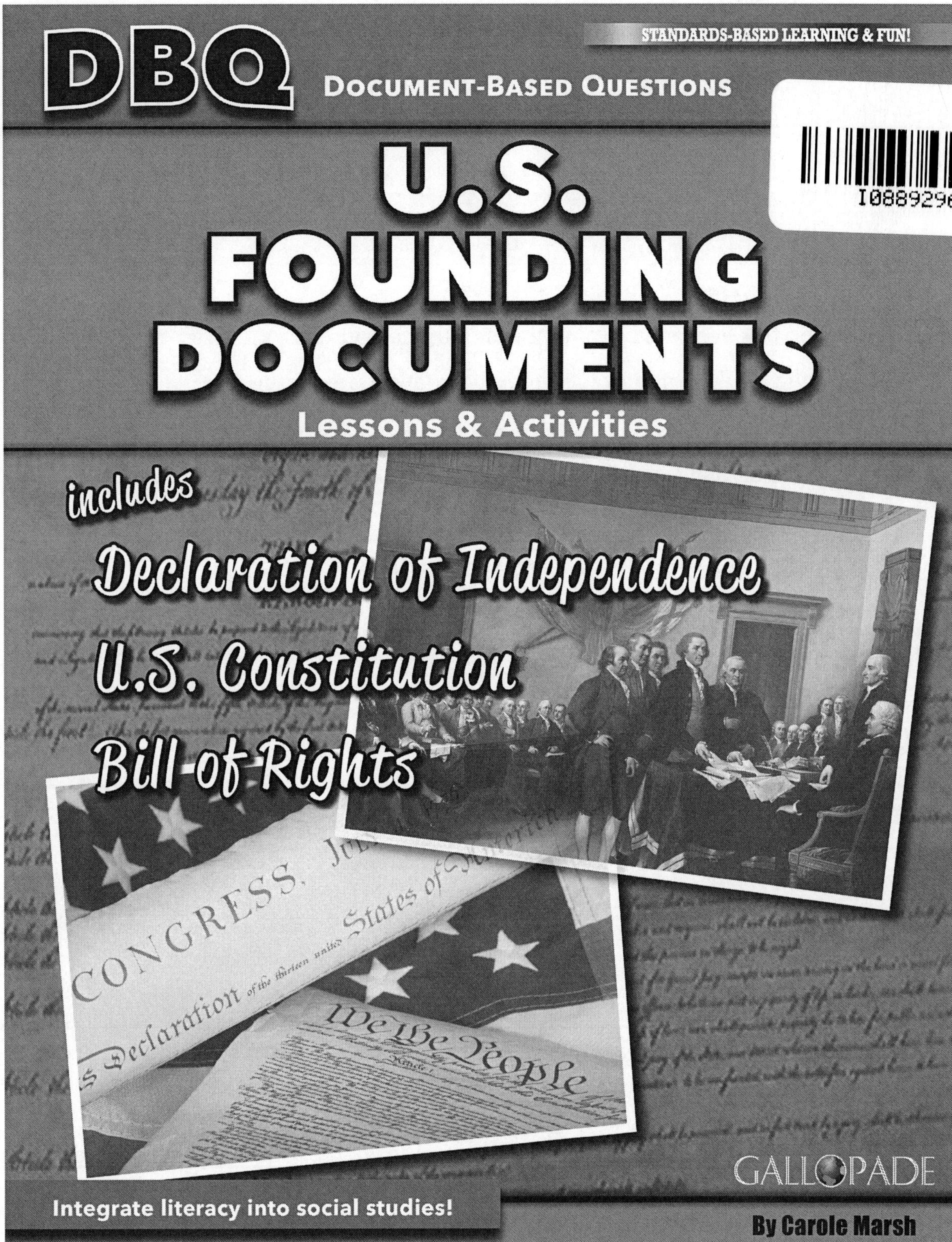
STANDARDS-BASED LEARNING & FUN!
DBQ
DOCUMENT-BASED QUESTIONS
I0889296
U.S.
FOUNDING
DOCUMENTS
Lessons & Activities
includes
Declaration of Independence
U.S. Constitution
Bill of Rights
CONGRESS, July
States of America
Declaration of the thirteen united
We the People
GALLOPADE
Integrate literacy into social studies!
By Carole Marsh

DBQ

WHAT IS DBQ?

The overarching concept of **Document-Based Questions (DBQ)** is that students answer a "big question" by reading and analyzing multiple documents, AND they support their answer with evidence and examples from the sources.

This process involves:

- Analyzing information in multiple sources
- Considering the perspective of authors of those sources
- Applying knowledge of a topic to the information presented
- Making inferences
- Drawing conclusions
- Applying logical, higher-order thinking
- Formulating an answer to the question that is posed

Once students follow the process, they can present their answer in the form of a well-organized essay that clearly answers the question and that supports the answer with detailed evidence and examples from the sources. It's the culmination of what they study as presented on many high school EOC graduation tests, AP exams, etc.

DBQ Skills = Lifelong Achievement

The process is also a skill students will need and use to form reasoned opinions and to present evidence-based conclusions and arguments on any topic throughout the rest of their life. Such uses could include speaking out convincingly on a local issue, making a recommendation or strategy to a boss, or developing a hypothesis for a cure for a disease and the request for funding and resources to pursue it.

Forming an opinion, argument, or recommendation by analyzing information from a variety of sources, and then communicating it in such a way that others can follow and see the merit in your analysis, is a life-long skill that will help students make better decisions and be better able to influence others to do the same.

TEACH DBQ WITH GALLOPADE!

Each page in Gallopade's DBQ series guides students through the process of analyzing and drawing conclusions from sources and communicating what they learn.

Lessons provide practice through a wide variety of sources.

Primary sources include:

- Replications of authentic primary source documents
- Quotations
- Maps, charts, and graphs
- Journal entries
- Political cartoons
- Photographs and illustrations
- Letters and speeches

Secondary sources include:

- Reference books
- Encyclopedia entries
- Websites
- Textbooks
- And more!

As students **read, observe, think, infer, categorize, apply, predict, and conclude,** these analytical skills and strategies become familiar and used more and more effectively. Students develop an understanding of how to distinguish fact from opinion, identify perspective and bias, determine the authenticity and purpose of sources, and apply logical thinking, inference, and analysis to a variety of topics.

The **guided instruction** provided throughout the activities in the DBQ series gives students the analytical tools and experience needed to be prepared for independent success!

Teachers: At the end of each unit, you will find a page with two end-of-unit "big picture" DBQs. Students should use the various sources they have analyzed to answer the questions in the form of a well-organized essay.

DBQ

DECLARATION OF INDEPENDENCE

THE UNITED STATES CONSTITUTION

THE BILL OF RIGHTS

Document-Based Questions

LESSON & ACTIVITIES

The Declaration of Independence

The unanimous Declaration of the thirteen united States of America

EARLY INDEPENDENCE

Read the text and answer the questions.

Many factors limited Great Britain's control over the colonies. From the beginning, the colonists enjoyed a good amount of independence from King George III. The vast distance of the Atlantic Ocean between Britain and the colonies made communication difficult. Britain could not control the colonies directly, so it gave the colonies charters to form their own governments. However, the French and Indian War caused Britain to seek to increase its control over the colonies.

The French and Indian War was a small part of a much larger war between Britain and France called The Seven Years' War. In the colonies, British and colonial forces defended the colonies against the French and France's Indian allies. Britain and the colonists won in 1763, but the war was very expensive for Britain.

The British government had to raise money to replenish funds used for the war. Since Britain defended the colonies in the war, they decided to tax the colonies. They passed several "acts" to raise taxes on colonial goods. The Sugar Act of 1764 and the Stamp Act of 1765 charged taxes on sugar and paper goods, and the Townshend Acts of 1767 taxed many imported goods. These new taxes angered colonists. To make matters worse, the colonists did not have a representative in Parliament. Many colonists argued that "taxation without representation" was unfair.

When colonists protested, King George III decided that the colonists had too much freedom to create laws. Thus, he removed the colonial governments. Many colonists saw King George III as a tyrant and began to suggest complete colonial independence.

1. Use a dictionary to define the following words.
   A. charter ______________________
   B. tax ______________________
   C. representation ______________________
   D. tyrant ______________________
2. What factors allowed the colonists to have some independence from Britain before the French and Indian War? ______________________
3. Why did the British government think it necessary to tax the colonies? ______________________
4. In your own words, explain "taxation without representation." ______________________

DBQ

SONS OF LIBERTY & THE BOSTON TEA PARTY

Read the text and answer the questions.

The Sons of Liberty was an important group that supported independence from Great Britain. The first Sons of Liberty formed in Boston in 1765. They were a group of shopkeepers and artisans who were outraged by the Stamp Act. Their first protest in August 1765 provoked a violent mob attack on the house of Andrew Oliver, a Stamp Distributor for Massachusetts. By the end of the year, community leaders in every colony had formed a Sons of Liberty group. Their first and primary goal was to force Stamp Distributors to resign.

The Sons of Liberty often used symbols and political messages to provoke violence against British taxes and acts. However, their most effective messages were delivered in newsprint. Many of the members were printers or publishers. News of the Sons of Liberty's activities and beliefs was printed in nearly every colonial paper.

The most famous act of the Sons of Liberty occurred in Boston in December 1773. In protest of the Tea Act, the Boston Sons of Liberty dressed as Indians and boarded three East India Tea Company ships. Using tomahawks, they broke open the chests of tea and poured them into the Boston Harbor. The next morning, tea still floated on top of the water. Citizens and sailors manned small boats and sank the floating tea with paddles to prevent any tea from being recovered. British reaction was swift and forceful. In 1774, the British Parliament passed the Coercive Acts (Intolerable Acts), which closed Boston Harbor and brought the Massachusetts governments under British control.

1. What was the original purpose of the Sons of Liberty?

____

____

2. What methods did the Sons of Liberty use to oppose the British government? Which method was most effective?

____

____

3. Describe the Boston Tea Party from the point of view of a British royal governor. Include your opinion of the colonists and their actions.

____

____

4. Explain the relationship between the Boston Tea Party and the Coercive Acts. What sentence in the text supports your answer?

____

____

DBQ

THE BOSTON MASSACRE

Look at the engraving and answer the questions.

This engraving was produced by Paul Revere shortly after the Boston Massacre and printed for distribution in the colonies.

Courtesy of Library of Congress

1. Describe what you see. What details do you notice first? ______________________________
____
____

2. Identify the two groups of people shown. ______________________________
____

3. What can you infer about the person who created this engraving? Cite evidence to support your conclusion. ______________________________
____
____

4. Use a dictionary to define massacre. Does the word "massacre" accurately describe the image presented? ______________________________
____

LOYALISTS, NEUTRALISTS, & PATRIOTS

Read the text and fill in the graphic organizer by writing three opinion statements from the point of view of each colonist. An example has been provided.

The American Revolutionary War began in 1775, but that did not mean that all colonists were in agreement about declaring independence from Great Britain–they weren't! In fact, almost one-third of all colonists did not want independence at all!

Colonists who were loyal to King George III and against declaring independence were called loyalists. Loyalists had many reasons to remain faithful to Great Britain. Some loyalists wanted to keep British military protection. Other loyalists were still connected to Britain by family and history. Some colonists felt a strong sense of duty toward King George III. In fact, many colonists considered themselves British citizens instead of "American colonists."

Many colonists wished to remain neutral. Neutralists often valued independence but understood that Britain offered protection, government, and trade. They also were unsure about waging war.

Patriots, colonists who wanted independence, had many reasons to be unhappy with British rule. Many patriots were influenced by the writings of John Locke, who stated that men have the right to oppose unjust governments. The Sons of Liberty were the most famous group of patriots. They were not content with British taxes and longed for freedom from British rule. Patriots saw King George III as a tyrant who ruled unfairly, imposed unfair taxes, and used deadly violence against colonists in the Boston Massacre.

Loyalist	Neutralist	Patriot
1. King George III is our beloved king!	1. King	1. King
2. King	2. King	2. King
3. King	3. King	3. King

"PAYING THE EXCISE-MAN"

Look at the cartoon and read the text. Then answer the questions and complete the writing prompt.

This political cartoon was published in 1774, entitled "Paying the Excise-Man." The text was written by Lord North, the Prime Minister of Great Britain, to King George III.

Courtesy of Library of Congress

> The Americans have tarred and feathered your subjects, plundered your merchants, burnt your ships, denied all obedience to your laws and authority; yet so clement and so long forbearing has our conduct been that it is incumbent on us now to take a different course. Whatever may be the consequence, we must risk something; if we do not, all is over.
>
> — Prime Minister Lord North, defending the Coercive Acts

PART A: Look at the political cartoon and answer the questions.

1. Use a dictionary to define excise. Identify the "excise-man" in the cartoon.
____

2. What is happening in this cartoon? Use an online resource to describe the process of "tarring and feathering." ____
____

3. What can you infer about the cartoonist's opinion of British taxes? ____________________
____

4. What is the message of this political cartoon? What symbols or details does the cartoonist use to convey this message? ______________________________
____
____

PART B: Read Lord North's quotation and answer the questions.

1. What is Lord North's opinion of American colonists? Support your conclusion with evidence from the text. ____

____

____

2. Use a dictionary to define clement. How do the British view their actions toward the colonists? ____

____

____

3. What is the tone of Lord North's message to King George III? ____________________

____

4. What words or phrases help you identify the tone? ____________________

____

PART C: Compare and contrast the cartoon and the text.

1. Explain how the cartoon and text differ in point of view. ____________________

____

____

____

2. Does Lord North's description of the Americans accurately describe the Americans in the cartoon "Paying the Excise-Man"? Explain why or why not. ____________________

____

____

____

Writing Prompt:

Imagine you are the British "Excise-Man" in the cartoon. Write a short response explaining your point of view. Include your reaction to being "tarred and feathered."

____

____

____

____

____

____

"JOIN, OR DIE"

Analyze the cartoon and answer the questions.

This political cartoon was first published in 1754 and reproduced in 1765 as a symbol supporting the American Revolution.

Courtesy of Library of Congress

1. What is the main message of this cartoon and who is the intended audience?

2. Is the message stated directly or indirectly?

3. What symbols and words communicate that message?

4. Which colonies are represented?

5. Do you agree with the message presented? Explain.

6. From what political point of view is this cartoon depicted?

7. How does this picture relate to the Declaration of Independence?

DBQ

AUTHORS OF THE DECLARATION

Read the text and answer the questions.

Thomas Jefferson was a well-known politician at the time of the American Revolution. He is often called the "Father of the Declaration of Independence" because he was responsible for writing the document. However, Thomas Jefferson did not write it alone.

Congress selected a "Committee of Five," including Benjamin Franklin, Roger Sherman, Richard R. Livingston, John Adams, and Thomas Jefferson, to produce the Declaration of Independence. Thomas Jefferson and the committee took many ideas from other writers and thinkers. One of these writers was George Mason.

George Mason was an important politician who wrote the Virginia Declaration of Rights. He was influenced by John Locke, who claimed all people should have certain rights. These rights are known as natural rights, which are basic rights that Mason believed no government should deny. Mason included the right to "enjoyment of life and liberty... and pursuing and obtaining happiness..." Thomas Jefferson used George Mason's Declaration of Rights as a model when writing the Declaration of Independence. Mason's work also had an important influence on another major American document, the Bill of Rights.

1. A. Define natural rights as it is used in the text. ______________________________

   ____

   B. In your own words, give an example of a natural right. ______________________

   ____

   ____

2. Is "Father of the Declaration" a fair title for Thomas Jefferson? Why or why not?

   ____

   ____

3. How did George Mason's Virginia Declaration of Rights influence the Declaration of Independence? ______________________________________

   ____

   ____

4. Choose Benjamin Franklin, Roger Sherman, Richard R. Livingston, or John Adams. Use an online or classroom resource to find five important facts about that person. Share your facts with the class.

DBQ

STRUCTURE OF THE DECLARATION

Read the text and answer the questions.

The Declaration of Independence is a statement against British control on trade, government, and political representation. In fact, it says that the colonies are free from Parliament and King George III. Overall, the Declaration explains and justifies the colonists' independence and gives a straightforward list of reasons why the colonies separated from Great Britain.

The first section of the Declaration, called the Preamble, states that the American people, when necessary, have the right to declare independence. The second section explains the ideas behind the Declaration. According to the Declaration, everyone has "certain unalienable rights," including "Life, Liberty, and the pursuit of Happiness." It says that the purpose of government is to protect those natural rights. In addition, people can change or oppose their government if those unalienable rights are in danger.

The third section is a long list of the colonists' complaints against King George III, including taxation and unfair trials. The fourth section claims that the colonists tried to find solutions and make peace. The fifth section restates the colonists' determination to defend their independence and rights. The last section is a list of signers representing all 13 colonies. Congressional delegates signed the Declaration to show the commitment of the colonies to protecting independence from Great Britain.

1. What is the purpose of the Declaration of Independence? ____________________

2. Describe the five main parts of the Declaration of Independence, not including the signers. ____________________

3. From the text, what is the key purpose of a government? ____________________

4. According to the Declaration, when do people have the right to oppose an oppressive government? ____________________

5. Explain the purpose of the fourth section. Why might the colonists have included it?

KEY PHILOSOPHY

Read the text and answer the questions.

The Declaration of Independence clearly states the colonists' purpose and reasoning for separating from the British monarchy. However, the ideas and philosophy behind the Declaration are not original to America. Thomas Jefferson admitted that the ideas were borrowed from other sources, including from John Locke, an English philosopher.

The Declaration includes several key ideas from John Locke's *Two Treatises of Government*. Locke thought that government should protect people's rights. Locke believed that government should be given power by the people—government should not take power. This idea would later be called popular sovereignty. Locke also thought that people could change any government that threatens the people's unalienable rights. Those natural rights, especially for Locke, included the right to "life, health, liberty, or possessions" (Locke). Jefferson then changed the statement to "Life, Liberty, and the pursuit of Happiness" (Declaration of Independence).

Locke's *Two Treatises of Government* expressed the idea that all men are free, equal, and allowed to protect their "unalienable Rights." Therefore, if men are free, they should not be forced to live under a tyrant. The drafters of the Declaration strongly claimed that British acts were denying them their unalienable rights.

1. Make a list of Locke's beliefs and summarize them in your own words. ____________

2. How did Locke's *Two Treatises of Government* influence the Declaration of Independence? ____________

3. Use the text to define popular sovereignty. How did the colonists use this concept to argue for independence from King George III? ____________

4. According to John Locke's philosophy, when is it necessary to change one's government? ____________

5. Use a Venn diagram to compare and contrast the unalienable rights according to John Locke's writing and the Declaration of Independence.

DBQ

THE BRITISH PERSPECTIVE

Read the text and answer the questions. Then complete the graphic organizer.

The colonists listed many complaints against the King, but King George III had a different point of view. For King George III, the Declaration of Independence was a clear sign of disrespect and defiance. Britain had recently defended the colonies during the French and Indian War. British Parliament thought a small tax on certain goods was a small price to pay for the protection of the British army. Britain left a standing army on guard in the colonies to protect the colonists from French and Indian attacks, and acts of Parliament were meant to help govern the colonies. Additionally, the British considered the colonies property of Great Britain.

The British side of key events, such as the Boston Massacre and the Boston Tea Party, tells a different side of history. British accounts of the Boston Massacre claimed that the massacre was an accident. They also accused the colonists of violently provoking and attacking British guards. When the Sons of Liberty threw British tea into Boston Harbor, British companies lost a large profit. The colonists' attempts at independence, including self-government and independent trade, angered the British government. The Declaration of Independence was final proof of colonial disrespect toward Great Britain and King George III.

1. Why did Great Britain leave a standing army in the colonies? ______________________
____
____

2. How did the Boston Tea Party affect the British? ______________________
____
____

Issue	British Point of View
Taxation	
Standing Army	
Boston Tea Party	
Boston Massacre	
Declaration of Independence	

DBQ

KEY DECLARATION EXCERPTS

Rewrite each excerpt to complete the chart. Use the completed chart to answer the questions.

Declaration Excerpts:	Rewrite in your own words:
"We hold these truths to be self-evident, that all men are created equal, that they are endowed by their Creator with certain unalienable Rights…"	
"That whenever any Form of Government becomes destructive of these ends, it is the Right of the People to alter or to abolish it, and to institute new Government..."	
"A Prince whose character is thus marked by every act which may define a Tyrant and is unfit to be the ruler of a free people..."	

1. Look up the definition of the following words and write a synonym for each.
   A. self-evident ____________________
   B. endowed ____________________
   C. abolish ____________________
   D. tyrant ____________________
2. What truths are considered "self-evident" according to the first excerpt? ____________________
3. What government is being described in the second excerpt? ____________________
4. What can you infer about the colonists' opinion of King George III from the third excerpt?

DBQ

LIST OF COMPLAINTS

The Declaration of Independence was a formal announcement to King George III that the colonists were separating from Great Britain. The colonists included a list of 27 complaints against King George III to make clear the reasons for separation.

Ten of the colonists' major complaints are listed below. Read each complaint and use the chart to rewrite each complaint from the perspective of a colonist. Two examples have been given. Use a dictionary to look up unfamiliar words. Then answer the questions.

1. For Quartering large bodies of armed troops among us
2. He has obstructed the Administration of Justice, by refusing his Assent to Laws for establishing Judiciary powers
3. For cutting off our Trade with all parts of the world
4. For depriving us in many cases, of the benefits of Trial by Jury
5. For transporting us beyond Seas to be tried for pretended offenses
6. For taking away our Charters, abolishing our most valuable Laws, and altering fundamentally the Forms of our Government
7. He has plundered our seas, ravaged our Coasts, burnt our towns, and destroyed the lives of our people
8. He has dissolved Representative Houses repeatedly, for opposing with manly firmness his invasions on the rights of the people
9. He has forbidden his Governors to pass Laws of immediate and pressing importance... till his Assent should be obtained; and when so suspended, he has utterly neglected to attend to them
10. He has abdicated Government here, by declaring us out of his Protection and waging War against us

1. Circle any words and phrases generally having a negative connotation.
2. What can you infer about the colonists' opinion of King George III? What words and phrases support your conclusion? ______________________________

____
____
____
____
____

#	What each complaint means to me
1.	The King put BRITISH soldiers in OUR homes!
2.	There is no justice under the King! He has dissolved our laws and courts.
3.	
4.	
5.	
6.	
7.	
8.	
9.	
10.	

DBQ

CREATED EQUAL?

Read the text and answer the questions in paragraph form.

The Declaration of Independence states, "all men are created equal." It also claims that all men are given certain unalienable rights. However, in early American history, black men and women were not equal and had few rights. Thomas Jefferson himself owned approximately 200 slaves, and slavery was an important form of labor in the agricultural south until 1865.

Jefferson's first draft of the Declaration included a paragraph against slavery. He claimed that King George III had promoted the slave trade in America. In fact, at the outbreak of the American Revolution, Great Britain offered freedom to all slaves who would fight with the British against the colonies. Both southern and northern slaveholders wanted the paragraph against slavery removed. Slavery was a cheap form of labor for the colonies. When Congress reviewed the first draft on July 1, 1776, the section against slavery was removed.

Although the Declaration of Independence celebrates human rights and freedom, slavery existed in America until 1865. For approximately a century after the Declaration of Independence, African American men and women were denied their "unalienable Rights."

1. Why did the colonies want Thomas Jefferson to remove the paragraph about slavery? ____________________

2. Explain how Great Britain used slavery against the colonies. ____________________

3. Predict what might have happened if the Declaration of Independence specifically outlawed slavery in the United States. ____________________

4. In a well-organized speech, share your response to the question "If all men are created equal, why did slavery exist?"

5. In American history, women did not receive the right to vote until 1920. Is it possible that Thomas Jefferson meant "all MEN are created equal," while excluding women? Discuss your thoughts as a class.

DBQ

INFLUENCE OF THE DECLARATION

Read the text and answer the questions.

The Declaration of Independence has had a lasting influence in U.S. history. In many cases, the Declaration of Independence has been used to support civil and human rights in the United States. Abolitionists, such as Frederick Douglass, used the Declaration to argue that slavery is unjust and that "all men are created equal." Elizabeth Cady Stanton and other supporters of women's equality used the Declaration of Independence to write their Declaration of Sentiments. Additionally, the Confederacy used the Declaration as a model for declaring secession from the Union.

The U.S. Declaration of Independence has also been influential in the history of other countries. After the U.S won its independence from Great Britain, other countries saw opportunity to claim their unalienable rights. Most notably, the leaders of the French Revolution in 1789 admired the colonists' struggle against an oppressive British government. The French Declarations of the Rights of Man and of the Citizen contains similar language and content to the Declaration of Independence. Additionally, the U.S. Declaration provided an example for officially declaring a new government. Several countries that declared independence, including Haiti, Venezuela, and Vietnam, modeled their declarations of independence after the U.S. Declaration.

1. What is the main idea of the text? ______________________________

____

2. How is the main idea developed and supported? ______________________________

____

____

3. Write an appropriate subtitle for each paragraph. ______________________________

____

____

4. List three ways the Declaration of Independence affected United States history.

____

____

____

5. According to the text, what qualities of the U.S. Declaration influenced the French Revolution? ______________________________

____

END-OF-UNIT DBQs

Use multiple sources to answer one of these end-of-unit questions in a well-organized essay.

1. **Why did the American colonies declare their independence from Great Britain?**
2. **What did the Declaration of Independence achieve, and how?**

Steps to follow:

1. Read each DBQ and briefly consider how you might respond to it. Then decide which question you want to answer in your essay.
2. Write a couple of quick ideas for a thesis statement. These are just tentative ideas to help you think about how you might answer the question.
3. Review the documents. As you do, list facts and examples that could help you answer the question you selected. In your notes, identify which document provided each fact or example.
4. Read your tentative thesis statements and choose one or write a new one. Read it again and improve upon it as needed.
5. Turn your notes into an outline of how you plan to organize your essay.
6. Write your essay. Use your notes and outline, and refer to the documents as needed.
7. Edit your essay. See "Essay Writing Tips" for things to check when editing.
8. Proofread your essay, make sure it's neat, be sure your name is on it, and turn it in!

Essay Writing Tips

- Catch your reader's interest at the start of your essay.
- Make sure your thesis statement is a strong, clear statement that states your overall answer to the DBQ.
- Include supporting evidence from at least three different documents. Don't just list facts—explain how analysis of the sources supports your thesis.
- Provide details to cite and add context to sources used to support claims. (For example, who said it, when, where, and to whom?)
- Include words to help your reader identify key points that support your thesis, connect claims with evidence, and transition between ideas.
- Edit and proofread your work before you turn it in!

DBQ

Document-Based Questions

LESSON & ACTIVITIES

The United States Constitution

The supreme law of the United States

DBQ

ARTICLES OF CONFEDERATION

Read the text and answer the questions.

The Articles of Confederation are known as the first U.S. Constitution. They were a list of rules meant to govern and unify the states. The Articles were ratified by all 13 states in March 1781, five years after the Continental Congress first began writing them.

The Articles were written on the heels of America winning the Revolutionary War against Great Britain. Therefore, it is no surprise that the Articles reflected a fear of big government. The Articles provided for a weak central government and gave considerable power to the states.

The Articles of Confederation gave the Continental Congress power to make laws but not the power to enforce them. The legislature had to get unanimous approval from all states to pass any laws—a difficult task because the states did not often agree.

James Madison believed the Articles were not strong enough. Only a strong central government, he felt, could support the nation and defend it. Spain and Great Britain were still a threat, the economy was suffering, and states were turning against each other.

Madison believed that states should be given power—just not to the detriment of the nation as a whole. He wrote: "Let it be tried whether any middle ground can be taken which will at once support a due supremacy of the national authority."

From May to September 1787, delegates to the Constitutional Convention in Philadelphia met to revise the Articles. George Mason, a delegate from Virginia, wrote: "The eyes of the United States are turned upon this Assembly and their Expectations raised to a very anxious Degree."

PART A: Use the text to infer whether each statement is **true** or **false**. Write **T** for true and **F** for false. Correct all false statements.

1. ______ Work on writing the Articles of Confederation began in 1781.

____

2. ______ The Articles of Confederation were the first U.S. Constitution.

____

3. ______ Congress could pass laws with a simple majority of votes.

____

4. ______ The purpose of the convention was to revise the Articles.

____

DBQ

PART B: Use a dictionary or context to define each word or phrase as it is used in the text.

1. on the heels of ______________________________

2. unanimous ______________________________

3. detriment ______________________________

4. middle ground ______________________________

PART C: Read the quotation. Explain what the quotation means in your own words.

1. "The eyes of the United States are turned upon this Assembly and their Expectations raised to a very anxious Degree." ______________________________

____

____

____

PART D: Determine whether each statement is **fact** or **opinion**. Write **F** for fact and **O** for opinion.

1. ______ The United States adopted its first written constitution in 1781.

2. ______ A big central government is a threat to the rights of all states.

3. ______ The Continental Congress could make laws, but the Articles did not give Congress the power to enforce them.

4. ______ The nation could not be defended from foreign attack without a strong central government.

5. ______ Spain and Great Britain were still a threat.

BONUS: Answer the following questions.

1. Explain why the authors of the Articles of Confederation favored a weak central government and gave power to the states. Cite evidence from the text to support your answer. ______________________________

____

2. What were the obstacles Congress faced under the Articles of Confederation? Explain how these obstacles made it difficult for the Congress to run the country. ______________

____

____

____

CONSTITUTIONAL CORRESPONDENCE

These texts are paraphrased excerpts from longer letters between John Jay and George Washington in 1786 on the topic of revising the Articles of Confederation.

Read the texts and answer the questions.

> Our national government has some very real problems that threaten "to blast the fruit we expected from our 'Tree of Liberty'." More and more of our leaders in government have the opinion that a General Convention is needed to revise the Articles of Confederation. Whether the people are ready for this or not is anyone's guess.
>
> John Jay to George Washington—March 16, 1786
>
> I absolutely agree with you, Sir, that the government is facing some real challenges. I would be surprised if a solution existed at this time. This situation is serious, but I fear that the people are not ready to make changes. I doubt that a Convention would make a difference. There is no doubt in my mind, however, that the Articles need revising. Something must be done—and fast!
>
> George Washington to John Jay—May 18, 1786

1. What is the meaning of John Jay's expression "to blast the fruit we expected from our 'tree of liberty' "? Is it positive or negative? ____________________

2. What is the common theme shared by both letters? Cite specific statements from the text to support your answer. ____________________

3. On what fact do both John Jay and George Washington agree? Cite specific statements from the texts to support your answer. ____________________

4. Compare and contrast the attitudes of the authors on holding a general convention. Cite specific phrases that support your conclusions. ____________________

DBQ

FEDERALISTS V. ANTIFEDERALISTS

Read the text, complete the graphic organizer, and answer the questions.

In the late 1700s, the young country was divided over the issue of a new Constitution. Most politicians were Federalists. They recognized that the Articles of Confederation were weak. They wanted a constitution with a stronger central government that could regulate the activities of the states. Generally, Federalists were wealthier aristocrats. On the other hand, some politicians were Antifederalists. Antifederalists were typically of a lower class. They feared state regulation and worried that a central government could easily abuse its powers. The Antifederalists' strongest argument against ratifying the Constitution was a lack of a bill of rights.

The final draft of the Constitution, sent to the states for approval, favored a strong central government. Federalists thought a central government could more easily compete in the world market, protect the nation from foreign threat, and unify the states. However, Federalists compromised with Antifederalists to limit the government's power. Thus, the Constitution includes a separation of powers, a system of checks and balances, and a bill of rights.

1. How did Federalists and Antifederalists feel about a strong central government? Complete the graphic organizer.

Federalists:	**V.**	**Antifederalists:**

2. According to the text, what benefits come from having a strong central government? Predict what problems might arise without a strong central government. ______________

____

____

____

____

____

____

DBQ

THE GREAT COMPROMISE

Read the text and answer the questions.

The delegates to the 1787 Constitutional Convention had to decide how individual states would be represented in Congress.

The Virginia Plan proposed a bicameral legislature, which included two houses of Congress. The number of representatives in each house would be based on proportional representation. This meant that a state's population determined how many representatives it would have in Congress. Delegates from populated states would be well represented, while small states like Delaware believed they would be underrepresented in Congress. To small states, this plan was a direct threat to their states' rights. They believed they would be out voted on issues that were important to them. They wanted more from this new Constitution!

William Paterson of New Jersey proposed the New Jersey Plan that included a unicameral legislature. This plan gave each state equal representation. The plan would leave most of the Articles of Confederation in place, but it would give Congress more power.

The New Jersey Plan was rejected in favor of the Virginia Plan, but delegates from the small states threatened to leave the Convention. Debate continued until July 16, when a compromise was finally reached.

The Great Compromise, proposed by Roger Sherman of Connecticut, blended the Virginia and New Jersey Plans. It was the perfect solution to many. The compromise stated that Congress would be made up of a Senate and a House of Representatives. Each state would have an equal number of Senators, but the number of representatives in the House of Representatives would be based on a state's population.

Both large and small states agreed to the Great Compromise and the first article of the Constitution was written to divide the legislative branch into the Senate and the House of Representatives. This solution is still in use today.

PART A: Use the text to infer whether each statement is true of the Virginia Plan or the New Jersey Plan. Write **V** for Virginia Plan and **N** for New Jersey Plan.

1. ______ The plan proposed a unicameral legislature.
2. ______ Both Houses of the legislature would be based on population.
3. ______ The plan was popular with small states.

PART B: Answer the questions related to the text's vocabulary.

1. What is meant by states' rights? Whose state's rights were most threatened by the Virginia Plan? ______________________________

____

____

DBQ

2. Define proposed. List several synonyms. ____

____

____

3. Which words and phrases in the text help define the meaning of proportional representation? Why did small states oppose it? ____________________________________

____

____

4. Summarize the key difference between unicameral and bicameral. __________________

____

____

5. Use a dictionary to define compromise. What part of speech is it as used in the text?

____

____

PART C: Read each statement and determine whether a small state or a large state was most likely to have said it. Write **S** for small state and **L** for large state. Use the text to help determine your answer.

1. ______ "A bicameral legislature with representation based on population in both houses of Congress is the best for all states!"

2. ______ "This plan is a direct threat to states' rights. We will be underrepresented in Congress!"

3. ______ "They say they will be outvoted in Congress, but what they are really looking for is power!"

4. ______ "At least one of the houses should have equal representation for every state!"

PART D: Read the statement made by Benjamin Franklin during the Constitutional Convention on the issue of state representation. What concept is he suggesting? Cite evidence from the text to explain how his statement applies to the state representation solution.

5. "When a broad table is to be made, and the planks do not fit, the artist takes a little from both, and makes a good joint." ____

____

____

____

____

DBQ

PURPOSE OF THE CONSTITUTION

Read the text and answer the questions.

In 1789, the Constitution was ratified without any amendments. Initially, the Constitution created the office of the President, established the Supreme Court, and allowed Congress to create laws, levy taxes on the people, and defend the country. The Constitution also gave all citizens equal rights in every state and allowed trade throughout the country. Overall, the Constitution created a stronger central government than allowed by the Articles of Confederation.

The Constitution was also written to give power to the people. The Preamble to the United States Constitution begins with three words: "We the People." These words may seem insignificant, but they are very meaningful! They indicate that the government's power comes from people who vote and contribute to the political government. The idea that people rule the government, and not the other way around, is called popular sovereignty.

When the Constitution was written, the colonies had only recently won their independence from Great Britain to become independent states. They did not want to create a government that would take away their rights like King George III had done. By giving power to the people, the Constitution helped create a limited government. The Constitution protects the rights of the people and limits the power of the government to control the people.

These limitations on government were important to many Constitutional delegates who were afraid of a powerful central government. Some states only ratified the Constitution on the condition that a bill of rights would be added later to protect individual and state freedoms. In December of 1791, the first ten amendments to the Constitution (The Bill of Rights) were ratified by all 13 states and became law. Today, the U.S. Constitution is made up of 7 articles and 27 amendments.

PART A: Use the text to infer whether each statement is **true** or **false**. Write **T** for true and **F** for false.

1. ______ The Constitution was ratified without a bill of rights.

2. ______ The Constitution gave the Supreme Court the power to create laws and taxes.

3. ______ The Preamble to the Constitution gives the government unlimited powers over the people.

4. ______ The Bill of Rights was ratified to protect the freedoms of states and individuals from the central government.

DBQ

PART B: Use information from the text to answer the questions.

1. What is the main idea of the first paragraph?

2. List the parts of government created by the Constitution.

3. What powers were given to Congress by the Constitution?

4. Use the text to explain the concept of popular sovereignty.

5. Explain the relationship between popular sovereignty and limited government. Cite evidence from the text to support your answer.

6. How did the recent events of the American Revolution influence the purpose of writing the Constitution?

7. Why might it be important that all citizens in every state have equal rights?

PART C: Complete the writing and speaking activities.

1. Write an essay on the topic, "We the People." In your own words, explain the importance of popular sovereignty in the United States. Proofread and edit your work.

2. Imagine that you are part of a committee presenting the U.S. Constitution to the people of America for the first time. In your own words, write a short speech explaining the purpose of the Constitution and the powers that it gives. Present your speech and answer any questions about the new Constitution.

ARTICLE I

These excerpts from the first article of the Constitution describe the basic organization and qualifications of the Legislative Branch.

Read the text and answer the questions.

Article I excerpts

1) "All legislative Powers herein granted shall be vested in a Congress of the United States, which shall consist of a Senate and House of Representatives."

2) "The House of Representatives shall be composed of Members chosen every second Year by the People of the several states.... Representatives and direct Taxes shall be apportioned among the several States... according to their respective [population]..."

3) "No Person shall be a Representative who shall not have attained to the Age of twenty five Years, and been seven Years a Citizen of the United States..."

4) "The Senate of the United States shall be composed of two Senators from each State, chosen by the Legislature thereof for six Years and each Senator shall have one Vote."

5) "No Person shall be a Senator who shall not have attained to the Age of thirty Years, and been nine Years a Citizen of the United States..."

1. What is the purpose of Section 1? Infer the meaning of "legislative Powers." ____________________

2. A. What is the minimum age requirement to be elected to the House of Representatives? What is the minimum age for a Senator? ____________________

   B. How often are Senators elected into office? How often are House Representatives elected into office? ____________________

3. Explain how Roger Sherman's Great Compromise directly influenced Article I of the Constitution. ____________________

4. In your opinion, why must a member of Congress first be a U.S. citizen? ____________________

DBQ

THE PREAMBLE

The Preamble to the Constitution was carefully worded by the delegates to the 1787 Constitutional Convention. The Preamble reveals the determination of the framers of the Constitution to avoid the same problems the states encountered under the Articles of Confederation.

Read the Preamble to the U.S. Constitution. Write each underlined phrase in the Preamble above the problem it addresses.

Preamble

We the People of the United States, in Order to form a more perfect Union, establish Justice, insure domestic Tranquility, provide for the common defense, promote the general Welfare, and secure the Blessings of Liberty to ourselves and our Posterity, do ordain and establish this Constitution for the United States of America.

1. ______________________________
   Under the Articles of Confederation, the central government had no power to defend U.S. citizens from attack or to protect its borders.

2. ______________________________
   Under the Articles of Confederation, the central government could not prevent problems between states, such as states placing tariffs on goods "exported" to other states.

3. ______________________________
   Under the Articles of Confederation, the central government could do little to protect the freedom the country had fought so hard for. Freedom for future generations was at stake.

4. ______________________________
   Article IV of the Articles of Confederation provided for an ineffective system of settling disputes between states because there was no national court system to interpret the laws.

5. ______________________________
   Under the Articles of Confederation, the central government had no enforceable system of taxation to raise money to provide services to its citizens.

DBQ

SEPARATION OF POWERS

Read the text and answer the questions.

The delegates at the Constitutional Convention in Philadelphia designed the new Constitution so that no branch of government would have too much power.

James Madison said, "The accumulation of all powers, legislative, executive, and judiciary, in the same hands, whether of one, a few, or many, and whether hereditary, self-appointed, or elective, may justly be pronounced the very definition of <u>tyranny</u>."

Articles I through III of the Constitution outline the powers and responsibilities of the three distinct branches of the U.S. government. The first article deals with the legislative branch, the second, the executive branch, and the third, the judicial branch.

The legislative branch consists of Congress, which is made up of the House of Representatives and the Senate. This branch is responsible for making the laws, levying taxes, and providing defense for the nation.

The executive branch is headed by the president and is responsible for enforcing the laws. The president has the executive veto power and is considered the Commander in Chief.

The judicial branch includes the Supreme Court and is responsible for interpreting the laws. The Supreme Court often sets important guidelines for how the laws are followed.

1. Use a dictionary to define <u>tyranny</u>. Summarize James Madison's quotation in your own words. ____________________

   ____

2. According to the text, what was the purpose of separating powers among different branches of government? ____________________

   ____

3. What historical events influenced the states to avoid the creation of a strong central government with no separation of powers? ____________________

   ____

4. In your opinion, does the separation of power help or hinder the government from making decisions? Why? ____________________

   ____

DBQ

SLAVERY AND COMPROMISE

Read the text and answer the questions.

During the 1787 Constitutional Convention, two major slavery debates were resolved through compromise.

The first compromise dealt with representation in Congress. Southern delegates to the Convention feared that the first draft of the Constitution did not give their states equal representation in Congress. Southern states had fewer citizens than northern states. Delegates from the South proposed allowing slaves to count toward their population. Northern delegates argued that slaves were property and shouldn't be counted toward a state's population.

The Three-Fifths Compromise allowed southern states to count three-fifths of their slaves toward their state's total population. A larger population meant more voting power in Congress.

The second compromise had to do with the slave trade and commerce. Primarily, Northern delegates wanted the slave trade to end, while many Southern delegates argued that slavery was vital to the region's economy. In addition, Southern delegates did not want Congress to impose tariffs on imported and exported goods because their economy was heavily reliant on trade. Northerners promoted tariffs because if imported goods were more expensive, people would buy U.S. products.

The Commerce and Slave Trade Compromise allowed Congress to tax imports (including slaves) but not exports. It also supported the slave trade for 20 years, after which Congress could ban it.

1. Explain why the Three-Fifths Compromise was important to the South. Predict the outcome had no compromise been made in Congress. ______________________________

____

____

____

2. Minister Samuel Hopkins wrote:

   "These States, who have been fighting for liberty... cannot agree in any political Constitution, unless it indulge and authorize them to enslave their fellow men..."

   Rewrite the quotation in your own words. Cite evidence from both compromises that supports Mr. Hopkins' observation. What do you think his opinion on slavery was? ______

____

____

____

DBQ

BILL OF RIGHTS QUOTATIONS

The final draft of the Constitution passed in Congress without a Bill of Rights. During the first Congress, James Madison urged his fellow congressmen to consider adding a bill of rights. These quotations are opinions about considering a bill of rights.

Rewrite each quotation in your own words to complete the graphic organizer and answer the questions.

Quotation:	What each quotation means to me:
"[A] bill of rights is what the people are entitled to against every government on earth, general or particular, and what no just government should refuse, or rest on inference." –Thomas Jefferson, Dec 1787	
"We owe it to these people. We didn't make it conditional. But we did make an honorable promise. We did agree to consider this issue in order to quell the fears of those who would otherwise support the Constitution. It is an important part of the democratic process to seek unity if possible. So I'm bringing it to you." –James Madison, 1789	

1. Identify the common theme between the two quotations. What words/phrases support your conclusion? ____

2. Summarize Jefferson and Madison's arguments for considering a bill of rights. How are they different? ____

3. In your opinion, which quotation is more persuasive? Explain. ____

DBQ

AMENDING THE CONSTITUTION

Read the text and answer the questions.

Amending the Constitution is an important process described in the U.S. Constitution. Article V of the Constitution lists two ways to amend the U.S. Constitution. The most popular method involves approval by the United States Congress and by the states.

Both houses of Congress (the Senate and the House of Representatives) must pass a proposal for an Amendment by a two-thirds majority. The proposal then goes on to the states for ratification.

Three-fourths of the state legislatures must pass the proposal before it can become an amendment. To pass a proposal in a state legislature requires only a simple majority of votes.

Historically, proposing and ratifying an amendment is a difficult process. Since 1789, over 11,000 proposals have been made to amend the Constitution. Only 27 proposals have been ratified by three-fourths of the state legislatures as amendments to the Constitution. The first ten amendments (Bill of Rights) were all proposed and ratified between 1789 and 1791.

1. Answer the following questions about vocabulary in the text.

   A. What is a synonym for proposal?

   B. Explain the meaning of ratification.

   C. Explain the difference between a two-thirds majority and a simple majority.

2. According to the text, what parts of the government are involved in ratifying amendments to the Constitution? Explain the process.

3. What is another name for the first ten amendments?

4. Why do you think the delegates of the Constitutional Convention thought it important to make the amendment process difficult? Explain.

5. Write a two-paragraph proposal suggesting your own amendment to the Constitution. Present your proposal to the class, debate any questions, and take a vote for ratification.

DBQ

A LIVING CONSTITUTION

Read the text and answer the questions.

Article V of the Constitution allows the Constitution to be amended (changed) if necessary. Since the inclusion of the Bill of Rights, the amendment process has allowed the United States to continually change and improve citizen's rights under the government. For many reasons, the Constitution is often called a "living document."

Excerpts from Amendments

13th Amendment (1865)
"Neither slavery nor involuntary servitude... shall exist with the United States, or any place subject to their jurisdiction."

15th Amendment (1870)
The right of citizens of the United States to vote shall not be denied or abridged by the United States or by any State on account of race, color, or previous condition of servitude.

16th Amendment (1913)
"The Congress shall have power to lay and collect taxes on income, from whatever source derived..."

19th Amendment (1920)
"The right of citizens of the United States to vote shall not be denied or abridged by the United States or by any State on account of sex."

1. Explain the significance of the 13th Amendment. How did it change United States history? ________________________

2. What power did the 16th Amendment give to Congress? How does this amendment affect the United States today? ________________________

3. Explain the relationship between the 15th and 19th Amendments. What group of people does each amendment affect? ________________________

4. In your own words, use the amendments to explain why the Constitution is considered a "living document." ________________________

DBQ

RATIFICATION OF THE U.S. CONSTITUTION

Use the map and data to answer the questions.

Ratification of the United States Constitution Results:

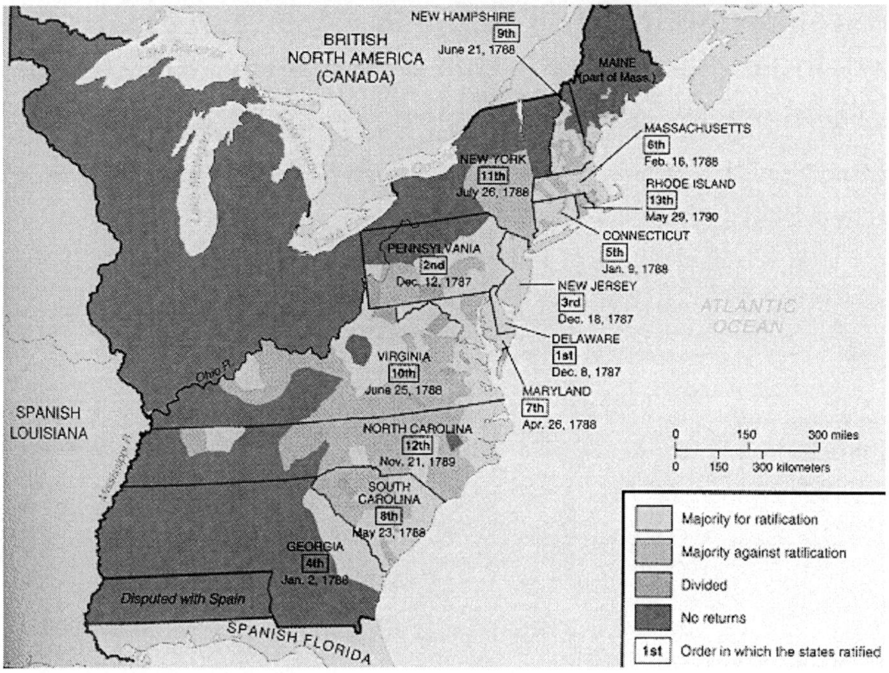

1. What do you notice about the boundaries of the thirteen states? ______________________

____

2. Which state was the first to ratify the new Constitution? Which state was last to ratify? What can you infer about these states? ______________________________________

____

3. At least a full two-thirds of the 13 states had to ratify the Constitution before it could go into effect. How many states were needed to ratify the Constitution, according to this rule? ____

____

4. Delaware is a small state. Predict how Delaware would have voted had the Great Compromise not been agreed upon by the delegates of the Constitutional Convention.

____

____

5. What does this map indicate about westward expansion at the time of the ratification of the Constitution? ____

____

DBQ

END-OF-UNIT DBQs

Use multiple sources to answer one of these end-of-unit questions in a well-organized essay.

1. **The Articles of Confederation were in effect fewer than ten years before being replaced by the U.S. Constitution. Why has the Constitution lasted ever since?**
2. **How does the U.S. Constitution preserve and protect democracy in the United States?**

Steps to follow:

1. Read each DBQ and briefly consider how you might respond to it. Then decide which question you want to answer in your essay.
2. Write a couple of quick ideas for a thesis statement. These are just tentative ideas to help you think about how you might answer the question.
3. Review the documents. As you do, list facts and examples that could help you answer the question you selected. In your notes, identify which document each fact or example comes from.
4. Read your tentative thesis statements and choose one or write a new one. Read it again and improve upon it as needed.
5. Turn your notes into an outline of how you plan to organize your essay.
6. Write your essay. Use your notes and outline, and refer to the documents as needed.
7. Edit your essay. See "Essay Writing Tips" for things to check when editing.
8. Proofread your essay, make sure it's neat, be sure your name is on it, and turn it in!

Essay Writing Tips

- Most essays start with an introductory paragraph that includes the thesis statement, followed by several paragraphs to support the thesis, and ending with a conclusion as the final paragraph.

What Is a Thesis?

A thesis is a sentence that clearly states what an essay will explain or prove. It includes a concise explanation of the logic, reasons, or key points that will be discussed. Examples:

- The reasons for exploration and colonization of the Americas can be summed up as The Three Gs: God, Gold, and Glory.
- The American Revolution was inevitable because of the universal desire of humans to be the masters of their own destiny.
- The physical environment had the largest impact on how American Indians lived, as evidenced by the food, clothing, and shelter of different groups throughout the Americas.

DBQ

Document-Based Questions

LESSON & ACTIVITIES

Bill of Rights

The first ten amendments to the U.S. Constitution, ratified in 1791 and guaranteeing such rights as the freedoms of speech, assembly, and worship

DBQ

FATHER OF THE BILL OF RIGHTS

Read the text and answer the questions.

George Mason did not particularly like politics, but he believed strongly in individual freedoms. When Britain began to unfairly tax the colonies before the American Revolution, George Mason got involved. He took George Washington's position in the Virginia Legislature so Washington could lead the Continental Army.

After the thirteen colonies declared their independence from Great Britain during the Revolutionary War, the new states began writing their state constitutions. George Mason wrote the Virginia Constitution. He also wrote the Virginia Declaration of Rights to protect the individual rights of Virginians. Other states soon did the same thing.

In 1787, the U.S Constitution replaced the old Articles of Confederation. The Articles had given the states a lot of power but gave little power to the federal government. Because of that, running the new government was difficult. To fix this problem, the new Constitution gave more power to the federal government.

As a result, George Mason urged his fellow delegates to add a bill of rights to the Constitution to protect individual freedoms. Many delegates did not agree. They argued that individual rights were already protected under state constitutions. Adding one to the U.S. Constitution seemed unnecessary.

To protest, George Mason refused to sign the Constitution. He argued that federal laws would supersede those of the states, taking away some rights of states and citizens. Two states, Rhode Island and North Carolina also refused to ratify the Constitution without a bill of rights. After much debate, the states agreed to sign the Constitution on the condition that a bill of rights was added later.

As promised, James Madison drafted a bill of rights during the first Congress. He borrowed ideas from George Mason's Virginia Declaration of Rights. The U.S. Constitution was amended to include the Bill of Rights (Amendments I-X) in December 1791. George Mason is honored with the title of "Father of the Bill of Rights" for his many contributions.

PART A: Use the text to infer whether each statement is **true** or **false**. Write **T** for true and **F** for false. Correct the false statements.

1. ______ George Mason served a minor role in the Virginia Legislature.
2. ______ George Mason wrote the Virginia Declaration of Independence.
3. ______ The purpose of a bill of rights is to protect individual rights and freedoms.
4. ______ Some states refused to ratify the U.S. Constitution without a bill of rights.
5. ______ George Mason was influenced by James Madison's ideas when he drafted the Bill of Rights.

PART B: Read the following quotation and explain how it supports George Mason's opinion about a bill of rights.

1. Excerpt from a letter to James Madison, concerning the lack of a bill of rights in the Constitution: *"...a bill of rights is what the people are entitled to against every government on earth...and what no just government should refuse..."* –Thomas Jefferson, December 1787

____

____

____

____

____

PART C: Answer the following questions about the text.

1. Explain how the Articles of Confederation and the new Constitution differed. What did this prompt George Mason to do? Explain why. ____________________

____

____

____

2. Some delegates argued that the U.S. Constitution did not need a bill of rights. What arguments did they use? ____________________

____

____

____

3. Define supersede as it is used in the text. Rewrite the sentence in the text using a synonym for supersede. ____________________

____

____

____

4. Cite two ways George Mason showed his disapproval when convention delegates refused to add a bill of rights to the Constitution. ____________________

____

____

____

5. Cite evidence from the text that supports the claim that George Mason is the "Father of the Bill of Rights." ____________________

____

____

____

____

DBQ

RIGHTS AND LIMITATIONS

The first ten amendments to the Constitution, also known as the Bill of Rights, were designed to protect individual rights and freedoms, while at the same time limiting the government's use of its power. The amendments are explained (paraphrased) below.

Read the summary of each amendment. Identify the main individual freedoms and/or limitations on government, and write them as they impact you on the graphic organizer. One amendment has been completed as an example.

I. Congress cannot make laws that limit a person's freedom of religion, freedom of speech, freedom to publish what he wants to, right to demonstrate peacefully with others, or right to ask the government to change something he doesn't like.

II. The government cannot take away the right of a person to carry or use a weapon to defend himself.

III. During peacetime, Congress cannot force a person to board soldiers; in wartime, they have to pass a law first.

IV. Citizens have the right to feel safe in their homes. No one can search a person's home, body, or things without a search warrant.

V. A person cannot be charged with a serious crime unless a grand jury says there is enough evidence for a trial. If a jury decides a person is innocent of a crime, that person cannot be tried again with a different jury for the same crime. A person does not have to testify against himself unless he wants to confess.

VI. A person who is arrested for a crime has the right to a speedy and public trial, with a jury of people in the area. A person has the right to know what he is accused of and who is testifying against him. A person has the right to a lawyer, even if he can't afford one.

VII. A person has the right to a jury trial in a federal civil case.

VIII. The government must not set unreasonable bail. When a person commits a crime, the punishment should not be cruel or unusual.

IX. People have rights, even the ones not listed in the Constitution.

X. In the Constitution, the powers that are not granted to the government are given to the states, or to the people.

#	Rights & Freedoms / Limitations on Government
I	
II	
III	
IV	I have the right to feel safe in my home. The government can't search my home without a warrant.
V	
VI	
VII	
VIII	
IX	
X	

1. Write a short essay explaining the purpose of the Bill of Rights.

2. As a class, debate which amendments are the most and least applicable to you. Discuss how your opinion might change as you get older.

THE FIRST AMENDMENT

The First Amendment to the U.S. Constitution guarantees protection of five individual rights. It also limits the government from making laws that infringe upon those rights.

Read the texts and answer the questions.

The First Amendment

"Congress shall make no law respecting an establishment of religion, or prohibiting the free exercise thereof; or abridging the freedom of speech, or of the press; or the right of the people peaceably to assemble, and to petition the government for a redress of grievances."

Most Supreme Court justices have agreed that the First Amendment is not without limits. Although the First Amendment protects the right to free speech, it does not protect speech that is untruthful, false, or dangerous to the security of the government. To summarize, the First Amendment has limitations on writing and saying things that are harmful to others; these are known as libel and slander. In addition, the First Amendment does not protect violent or forceful assembly.

1. List the five rights protected by the First Amendment. ______

2. Using evidence from the text, define libel and slander. ______

3. The First Amendment says that Congress cannot make laws that abridge, or limit, the freedom of speech. Does this mean that you can say anything you want any time you want? Write a short response, and use evidence from the text to support your argument. ______

4. What word in the First Amendment limits the people's right to assemble? ______

5. List the First Amendment rights in order of importance to you. Compare your list with other students' lists and discuss. ______

DBQ

THE SECOND AMENDMENT

The Second Amendment to the U.S. Constitution guarantees protection of people's right to keep and bear arms.

Read the text and answer the questions.

The Second Amendment

A well regulated militia being necessary to the security of a free state, the right of the people to keep and bear arms shall not be infringed.

1. Use a dictionary to define the following terms as they are used in the Second Amendment.
   A. militia ______________________
   B. keep ______________________
   C. bear ______________________
   D. arms ______________________
   E. infringed ______________________

2. Well regulated means "well trained." Why do you think the authors of the Second Amendment chose to write "a well regulated militia" as opposed to "a militia"?
____
____

3. According to the Second Amendment, what was the purpose for maintaining a regulated militia? ______________________
____

4. Use evidence from the text to support the statement, "The Second Amendment *protects* the right to keep and bear arms." ______________________
____
____

5. The right to own and bear arms was important to the first colonists and settlers who moved west. What reasons might early settlers have had to bear arms? Use an online resource to gather information. ______________________
____
____
____
____

DBQ

THE THIRD AMENDMENT

Read the texts and answer the questions. Then use the texts to complete the Problem-Solution organizer.

The Third Amendment

No Soldier shall, in time of peace be quartered in any house, without the consent of the Owner, nor in time of war, but in a manner to be prescribed by law.

The Third Amendment may seem unusual now, but when this amendment was written, soldiers would often stay in nearby homes. When the colonies were under British rule, Britain passed laws that forced American colonists to feed and find housing (empty barns, inns, bars) for the British troops. Later, the king enacted the Quartering Act of 1774 (one of the Intolerable Acts) to punish the American colonists for dumping British tea into Boston Harbor. The Act forced American colonists to quarter British troops—even in private homes! Not only was it a hardship to feed and house these troops, the colonists felt their privacy was being violated.

1. Use a dictionary to define quartered as it is used in the Third Amendment. ______________________________

2. What can you infer about the colonists' opinion of the Quartering Act of 1774? Cite evidence to support your conclusion. ______________________________

3. Re-create the graphic organizer on a separate sheet of paper. Use information from the text to identify the problems, solutions, and results of the Third Amendment.

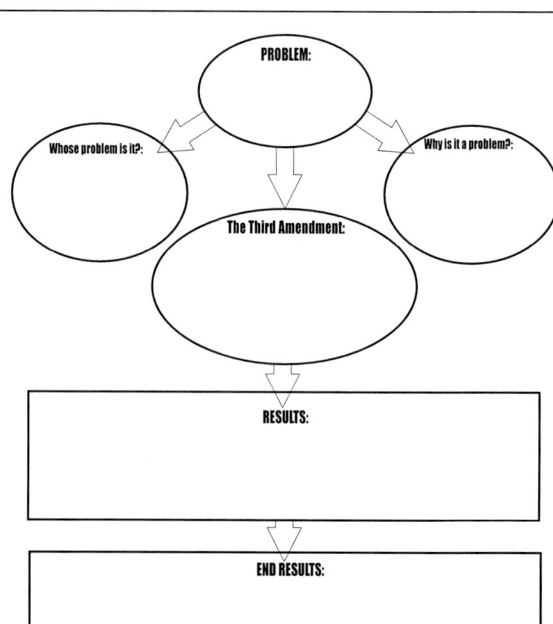

THE FOURTH AMENDMENT

The Fourth Amendment protects a person against unlawful searches and seizures. The following is a Supreme Court case involving the Fourth Amendment.

Read the text and answer the questions.

The Fourth Amendment protects our privacy. It states, "The right of the people to be secure in their persons, houses, papers, and effects, against unreasonable searches and seizures, shall not be violated, and no Warrants shall issue, but upon probable cause, supported by Oath or affirmation, and particularly describing the place to be searched, and the persons or things to be seized."

The 1927 Supreme Court case *Olmstead v. United States* involved a man by the name of Roy Olmstead. He was suspected of smuggling and selling alcohol during Prohibition, a time when it was against the law to distribute, make, and sell alcohol.

To gather evidence against Mr. Olmstead, police wiretapped his office phone without a warrant, or lawful permission. The Supreme Court ruled 5-4 that use of the evidence was allowable. Supreme Court Chief Justice Taft argued that wiretapping was not the same as a physical search and seizure as stated in the Fourth Amendment.

Supreme Court Justice Brandeis disagreed with the ruling. He argued that wiretapping is just as intrusive as opening someone's mail without permission. He supported his argument by citing how the Fourth Amendment protected a person's right to privacy.

1. A. Use an online dictionary to define intrusive. ______________________________

   ____

   B. Wiretapping is the act of monitoring or recording a phone call without permission. Explain how wiretapping is intrusive. ______________________________

   ____

2. Rewrite the Fourth Amendment in your own words. ______________________________

   ____

   ____

   ____

3. How did the Fourth Amendment apply in the Olmstead case? Cite evidence from the text to support the relationship. ______________________________

   ____

4. In your opinion, why is the Fourth Amendment important? Write a two-paragraph response explaining why the Fourth Amendment is important and predicting what might happen if the Fourth Amendment did not protect individuals from unlawful searches and seizures.

DBQ

THE FIFTH AMENDMENT

The Fifth Amendment makes sure that the rights of the accused are protected in the criminal justice system. A person accused of a crime has the right to 1) know his/her rights 2) receive due process, a fair trial by jury after evidence is collected, 3) not be charged with the same crime twice and 4) have a lawyer present during questioning.

Read the text and answer the questions.

In 1963, Ernesto Miranda was accused of a brutal crime and arrested. Police questioned him without first telling him his rights. Police used a signed confession to find him guilty in a court of law.

His lawyer tried to have the confession thrown out as evidence because he felt that police broke the law by failing to tell Mr. Miranda that he 1) didn't have to say anything that might be self-incriminating, and 2) had the right to an attorney during questioning. The lower court threw out Miranda's attorney's motion, or request, and allowed the confession as evidence in court.

The case was appealed to the Supreme Court. In *Miranda v. Arizona*, the Supreme Court agreed with Miranda's lawyer. The Court ruled that the confession could not be used as evidence, since Mr. Miranda was not told his rights before questioning.

Now, to better protect the rights of the accused, police are required to give a Miranda warning before questioning a person accused of a crime.

1. Use a dictionary to explain the difference between the meanings of incriminating and self-incriminating. Which type of testimony is limited by the Fifth Amendment?

___

___

2. Who do you have a right to have present when being questioned by police? ___

___

3. When a trial is not fair, or due process is not followed, the case can be appealed. Explain the meaning of appealed as it is used in the text. ___

___

4. Explain how the Fifth Amendment protected Mr. Miranda. ___

___

5. What are all police required to do as a result of the *Miranda v. Arizona* Supreme Court decision? What is the purpose of this requirement? ___

___

___

DBQ

THE SIXTH AMENDMENT

Read the text. Match the numbered phrases with their explanations in the chart.

The Sixth Amendment

In all criminal prosecutions, the accused shall enjoy the 1) right to a speedy and 2) public trial, by an 3) impartial jury of the 4) state and district wherein the crime shall have been committed, which district shall have been previously ascertained by law, and 5) to be informed of the nature and cause of the accusation; 6) to be confronted with the witnesses against him; 7) to have a required process for obtaining witnesses in his favor, and 8) to have the assistance of counsel for his defense.

#	Explanation
	Jurors must be unbiased, and will decide guilt or innocence based on evidence presented at the trial.
	Defendant has the right to know what he/she is accused of.
	Defendant has the right to not wait long in jail before the trial takes place.
	The trial must be held in a public court, not a secret location.
	Defendant has the right to know who his/her accuser is.
	The trial location will be held in the area where the crime took place.
	Defendant has the right to a lawyer, even if he/she cannot afford to pay for the lawyer's services.
	Defendant has the right to call witnesses to testify for his/her benefit.

DBQ

THE SEVENTH AMENDMENT

Criminal cases are protected by the Sixth Amendment, but civil cases, non-criminal cases, involving money from business, property, etc., are protected by the Seventh Amendment. A person seeking damages (money, property, etc.) from a defendant has the right to a jury trial in a federal court.

Read the text and answer the questions.

When the colonies were still controlled by Great Britain, colonists were not allowed to have a <u>jury trial</u>. Judges alone made decisions in civil trials. The judges were often corrupt and ruled unfairly. The Seventh Amendment, protecting the right to a jury trial in certain civil cases, protects people from this kind of abuse of power.

If the money involved in a case is more than a certain amount, a jury trial in federal court may be requested. First, though, the judge will encourage the parties involved to settle out of court due to the cost of a trial. If a settlement can't be reached, a jury trial can be scheduled.

The job of a judge in the jury trial is not to make the final decision, but to instruct the jury on the law and evidence that can be used. The jury decides if there is enough evidence. The jury then hands down a verdict and can award money in damages.

1. Use a dictionary to define <u>jury trial</u> as it is used in the text. ________________________

____

2. According to the text, why would a judge encourage two parties to settle an argument without a court trial? ________________________

____

3. Explain the relationship between the Sixth and Seventh Amendments. What is the difference between a civil trial and a criminal trial? ________________________

____

4. According to the text, what aspects of British control caused colonists to create the Seventh Amendment? ________________________

____

5. Compare and contrast the roles of the judge and the jury in a jury trial. What are the pros and cons of having a jury make decisions instead of a judge? ________________________

____

____

____

DBQ

THE EIGHTH AMENDMENT

Read the text, look at the illustration, and answer the questions.

The Eighth Amendment

Excessive bail shall not be required, nor excessive fines imposed, nor cruel and unusual punishments inflicted.

The cartoon shows a British colonial pillory, a form of public punishment.

1. Bail is a sum of money required for release from jail. What limitation does the Eighth Amendment put on bail? Why was this done?

____

2. Define cruel and unusual punishments in your own words. _______________

3. Explain how using a pillory stock could be considered cruel and unusual punishment. Cite details from the illustration. _______________

4. Like many of the Bill of Rights amendments, the Eighth Amendment was written to avoid some of the problems that existed during colonial times. Based on this statement, use the Eighth Amendment to make three inferences about the legal system when the colonies were ruled by Britain. _______________

DBQ

NINTH & TENTH AMENDMENTS

Amendments nine and ten of the Bill of Rights limit the power of the federal government and protect the rights not specifically listed in the Constitution.

Define the underlined words. Then complete the graphic organizer by using the chart to rewrite the amendments in your own words.

1. Use a dictionary to define the following words: enumeration, construed, deny, disparage, and retained.

The Ninth Amendment	Meaning
The enumeration in the Constitution, of certain rights,	
shall not be construed to deny or disparage others retained by the people.	

What the amendment means to me:

1. Use a dictionary to define the following words: delegated, prohibited, and reserved.

The Tenth Amendment	Meaning
The powers not delegated to the United States by the Constitution,	
nor prohibited by it to the States	
are reserved to the States respectively, or to the people.	

What the amendment means to me:

2. Compare and contrast the Ninth and Tenth Amendments. What is the purpose of each? Compare your response with a partner. ______________________________

3. Many delegates at the constitutional convention were against the Bill of Rights. They worried that by listing certain rights they would limit others. In your opinion, does the Bill of Rights limit other rights? Why or why not? ______________________________

DBQ

END-OF-UNIT DBQs

Use multiple sources to answer one of these end-of-unit questions in a well-organized essay.

1. Was a Bill of Rights necessary? Why or why not?

2. How did the tyranny faced by American colonists create lasting benefits that U.S. citizens enjoy today?

Steps to follow:

1. Read each DBQ and briefly consider how you might respond to it. Then decide which question you want to answer in your essay.
2. Write a couple of quick ideas for a thesis statement. These are just tentative ideas to help you think about how you might answer the question.
3. Review the documents. As you do, list facts and examples that could help you answer the question you selected. In your notes, identify which document each fact or example comes from.
4. Read your tentative thesis statements and choose one or write a new one. Read it again and improve upon it as needed.

Strategies for Analyzing Documents

- Compare and Contrast
- Categorize Information
- Determine Perspective
- Distinguish between Fact and Opinion
- Sequence Events
- Make Inferences
- Analyze Causes and Effects
- Predict Possible Outcomes

5. Turn your notes into an outline of how you plan to organize your essay.
6. Write your essay. Use your notes and outline, and refer to the documents as needed.
7. Edit your essay. See "Essay Writing Tips" for things to check when editing.
8. Proofread your essay, make sure it's neat, be sure your name is on it, and turn it in!